Copyright © 1999 by Nord-Süd Verlag AG, Gossau Zürich, Switzerland
First published in Switzerland under the title *Alle Wetter*
English translation copyright © 1999 by North-South Books Inc.

First published in the United States, Great Britain, Canada,
Australia, and New Zealand in 1999 by North-South Books,
an imprint of Nord-Süd Verlag AG, Gossau Zürich, Switzerland.

Distributed in the United States by North-South Books Inc., New York.

Library of Congress Cataloging-in-Publication Data is available.
A CIP catalogue record for this book is available from
The British Library.

ISBN 0-7358-1047-8 (trade binding) 10 9 8 7 6 5 4 3 2 1
ISBN 0-7358-1048-6 (library binding) 10 9 8 7 6 5 4 3 2 1
Printed in Belgium

For more information about our books,
and the authors and artists who create them,
visit our web site: http://www.northsouth.com

The idea of the weather frog is taken from European folklore.
German children know all about the weather frog and often
receive one as a gift, complete with a little jar with a ladder
inside. As with other similar weather superstitions involving
animals or insects, there is some meteorological validity to the
idea of a weather frog, since when the barometric pressure is
high (fair weather), insects would fly higher, sending a hungry
frog up the ladder. Conversely, when the barometer drops (a
harbinger of bad weather), the insects would fly lower, sending
the frog to the bottom of the jar.

Udo Weigelt

All-Weather Friends

Illustrated by Nicolas d'Aujourd'hui

Translated by J. Alison James

North-South Books / New York / London

Moss had just taken his morning bath when Hedgehog came by. "Good day," Moss said cheerfully.

"That's just what I came to find out," Hedgehog said.

"What do you mean?" asked Moss.

"Is it going to be a good day? Everyone says frogs can tell what the weather will be. The humans in the house at the edge of the woods even have a frog in a jar. It's their weather frog. I heard them say so."

Moss looked at Hedgehog in surprise. He'd never heard of such a thing.

"Ummm," he said slowly, while thinking fast. "Well, you see, yes, I believe the weather today will be fine. The sun will shine all day. It will be beautiful."

"Great!" cried Hedgehog. He wanted to go on a picnic with some other animals.

But no sooner had the animals set out than the sky suddenly grew dark. The first raindrops fell. Then a torrential storm sent the animals running for cover.

Everyone was furious. Moss had ruined their plans. He had promised them a sunny day. They headed down to the pond to give him a piece of their minds.

"You said it would be beautiful all day!" said Hedgehog accusingly.

"Yes, well, everyone makes mistakes," said Moss, turning red. "But now I know for sure: today it is going to rain. All day. You'd better stay home."

Just then the sun broke through the clouds. Within moments it was steamy and warm.

"What is wrong with you?" asked Beaver. "The sun is shining, but you just said that it was going to rain all day."

"One wonders," cracked Crow, "if you are a proper frog at all!"

Moss was very embarrassed. If everyone thought that frogs could predict the weather, then it must be true. But why on earth couldn't he do it?

"Of course I'm a proper frog," he said. "Today it will be partly cloudy, with a chance of afternoon showers."

But then it began to snow. Now the animals were really angry.
"You are a liar, Moss!" cried Fox, outraged. "Nothing you say is true!"
The animals turned up their noses and went away, leaving Moss confused and unhappy.

I really didn't mean to disappoint them, he thought. But how should I know what the weather is going to be? Especially on a day when it changes every five minutes. We've never had such weather before.

Still, the animals expect me to do it, Moss said to himself. So I'll have to learn. Surely that weather frog must be a professional and will be able to help me.

So Moss hopped off to the humans' house at the edge of the woods.

When he got there, the sun was shining brightly and all the snow had melted. On the windowsill stood a big glass jar. And in the jar sat a frog.

"Hello!" Moss said. "Could you perhaps tell me how one is supposed to know what the weather will be?"

The frog in the jar only stared at him unhappily, with wide unblinking eyes.

Moss tried a louder voice. "Hello! Can you hear me?"

This time the frog croaked something, but Moss couldn't hear through the glass. He hopped up on the windowsill, and the other frog grew quite excited. Suddenly Moss realized: This frog is imprisoned! I have to help!

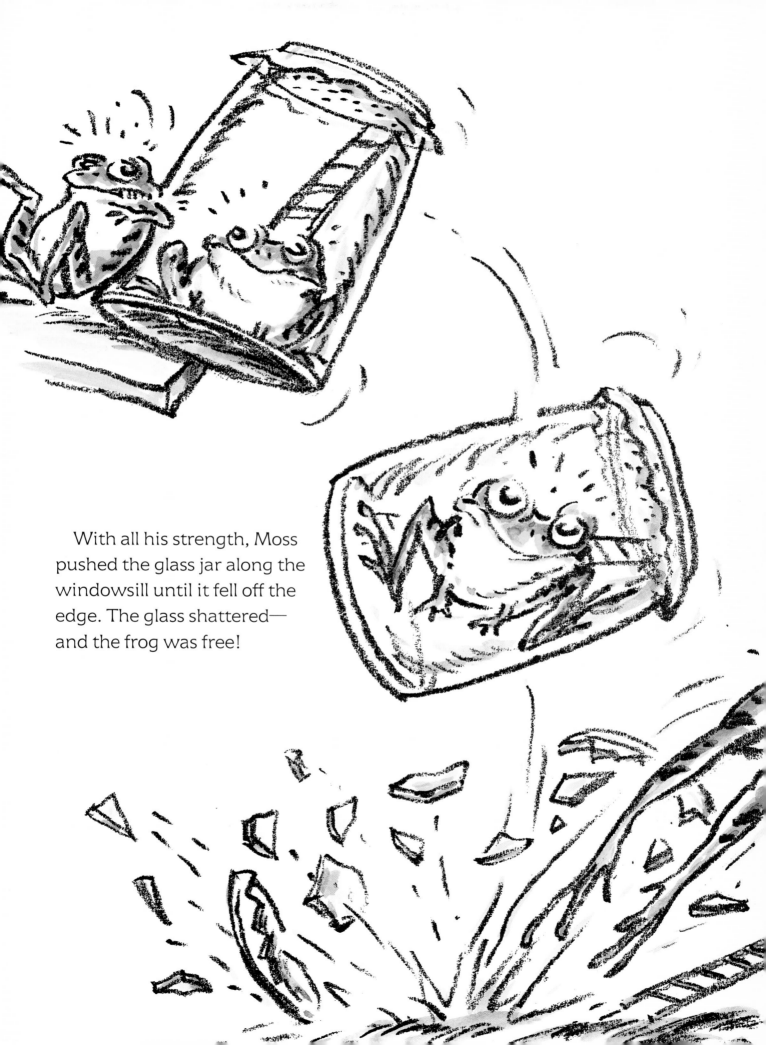

With all his strength, Moss pushed the glass jar along the windowsill until it fell off the edge. The glass shattered— and the frog was free!

The two frogs hopped away lickety-split.

They didn't pause until they reached the edge of the forest.

"Thank you for helping me escape," said the frog. "My name is Olive."

"I'm glad I came along," he said proudly. "I'm Moss. Why were you trapped in that glass jar with just a ladder?"

"Humans have an old saying that if a frog is up the ladder, there will be fair weather," explained Olive. "But frogs can't really forecast the weather."

"They can't?" Moss sighed, and he told her what had happened with the other animals.

"Why did you pretend?" asked Olive.

"They told me that all *proper* frogs knew how to predict the weather, so I had to show them that I really was one."

"Well, they were wrong," said Olive. "And you're lucky you didn't end up in a jar like me." Then she laughed. "Come on, let's play. We can do that in any weather."

They hopped all the way back to Moss's pond.

And then they played games,
like who could hop the highest

. . . who could inflate the fattest

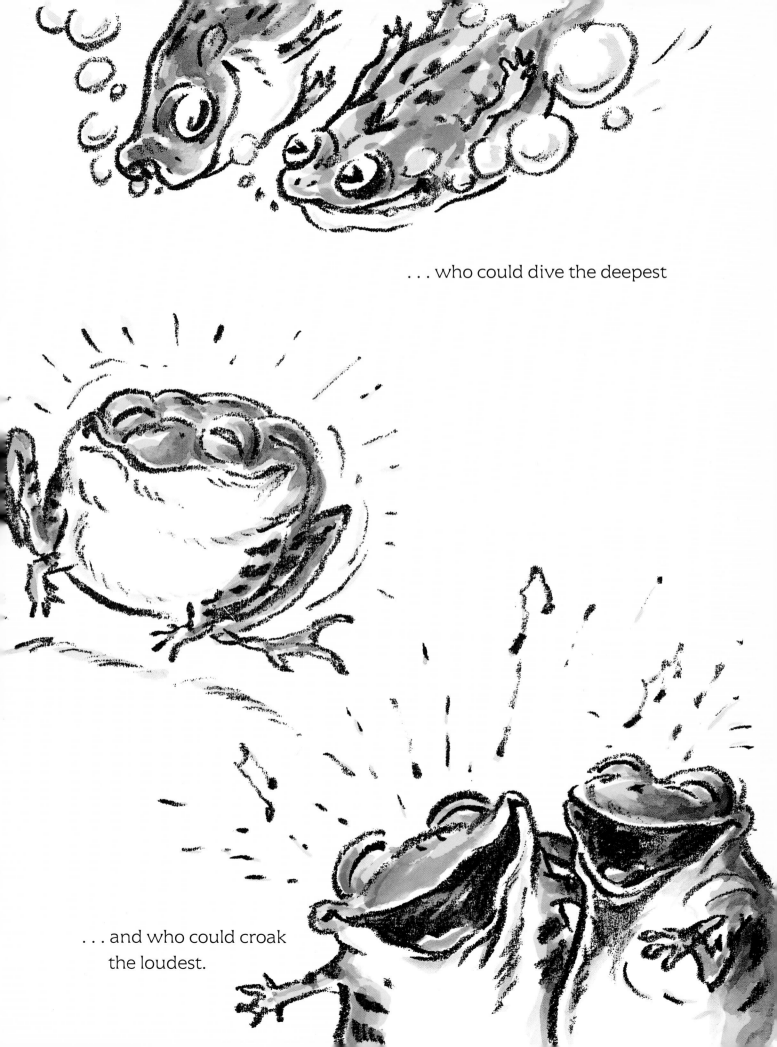

. . . who could dive the deepest

. . . and who could croak
the loudest.

When the other animals came back to the pond, they were surprised to see two frogs.

"Friends!" croaked Moss proudly. "I'd like you to meet the real weather frog. She was trapped in a jar and I rescued her."

All the animals started talking at once:

"What will the weather be?"

"Is it going to rain tomorrow?"

"Will we have a hot summer?"

"How much snow will fall next winter?"

Olive and Moss started laughing.

The animals grew quiet.

"I have absolutely no idea!" Olive declared.

The animals gasped.

"But," Olive continued, "I do have an idea how you can enjoy the weather, rain or shine."

"Tell us!" cried the animals.

"COME AND SWIM!" Moss and Olive cried. And KER-SPLASH! they jumped into the pond.

One by one the other animals followed.
And they were all having such a good time splashing about, they didn't even notice when it started to rain.